The Bird With No Wings

Learn Italian with Uccellino

Written by Franca Porreca   Illustrated by Aldila Permata

"Dedicated to everyone who has felt different at one time or another. You are perfect. You are enough."

Bird

Uccello
oo–chel–oh

**Mama Bird was very excited
because pretty soon her baby would hatch.**

She waited and waited until one morning,
the **egg** cracked and little Uccellino came out!

He was beautiful, but right away,
Mama Bird noticed something was not quite right.

Her **Baby Bird** was born with no wings!

She felt very, very **sad**.
She did not know how she could help her little bird.

Friends

Amici
ah–mi–chi

Then, she felt her motherly instincts kick in.
She gathered her closest bird **friends** together
and told them about her worries.

Help

Aiuto
ay—yoo—toe

Moments later, one bird announced, "I have an idea!
If every bird here donates a few of their feathers,
we can **help** make a set of wings for our friend."

Mama Bird was so thankful for this offer
and they all started to work together on the plan.

Soon they had a colorful set of wings for Uccellino
and they put them on him for the first time.

At first, Uccellino had a hard time trying to fly with his new wings. But he practiced with them every day for months.

"I'm never going to be able to fly with these wings, and I look **different** than the other little birds," he said with frustration.

Mama Bird looked him in the eyes and explained that being different from all the other birds only made him more special.

Fun

Divertimento
dee–ver–tee–men–toe

Uccellino thought about it, and he thought that his mama was probably right. That did sound more fun.

"Even when we feel like giving up, we have to keep going. Asking friends for their support always helps," Mama Bird said.

So Mama Bird called all of their bird friends back
and soon they had convinced Uccellino to get to the end
of the branch for one more attempt.

Fly

Volare
vo–lar–eh

He took a breath, puffed his chest, and with a big leap
he started flying and flying higher into the sky!

It was a miracle! The miracle of courage, kindness, cooperation, and friendship.

Finally, thanks to the help of his Mama and friends, the Bird With No Wings could fly.

A note about the author:

Franca Porreca was born in Italy where she learned the doctrine of Maria Montessori. She taught in Montessori schools in Italy before moving to the United States where she continued teaching for a total of 44 years. Franca's love for children has been her life's inspiration, passion, and work. After reading thousands of children's book, this is the first she has written.